This Book Belongs To:

_____
BROOKLYN BOOK BODEGA

*For Katali, to celebrate and be proud of your roots.
And for Naomi, who saw the potential in this story first.*

—S.C. and R.N.

*For my niece, Ava, may you always
know your story and celebrate it.*

—K.O.

My Smock Is a Story
Text copyright © 2024 by Reuben Nantogmah and Samantha Cleaver
Illustrations copyright © 2024 by Keisha Okafor
All rights reserved. Manufactured in Italy.
No part of this book may be used or reproduced in any manner whatsoever without written permission except in the case of brief quotations embodied in critical articles and reviews. For information address HarperCollins Children's Books, a division of HarperCollins Publishers, 195 Broadway, New York, NY 10007.
www.harpercollinschildrens.com

Library of Congress Control Number: 2023948730
ISBN 978-0-06-329395-3

The artist used Procreate to create the digital illustrations for this book.
Typography by Christy Hale
24 25 26 27 28 RTLO 10 9 8 7 6 5 4 3 2 1

First Edition

MY SMOCK IS A STORY

by **Reuben Nantogmah** and
Samantha Cleaver
illustrated by **Keisha Okafor**

HARPER
An Imprint of HarperCollinsPublishers

"Today is a special day," Dada says when he wakes me up.

"Why?" I ask.

"It's Auntie's wedding, and you'll get your first binŋmaa."

"What's a binn-ma?" I try hard to say it just right.

"Come, let me show you."

"These are my binŋmaa, my smocks," Dada says.

"We are Dagomba. Our ancestors have worn smocks since before you were born, before I came to America, before Ghana was a country."

The smocks in Dada's closet feel rough and bumpy. I push one away and it's like moving a heavy curtain.

"Each smock takes time to make," says Dada. "Master artisans weave yarn into fabric and fabric into cloth."

With our hands, we pretend we are weaving, over, under, over, under.

I giggle, watching us move in sync.

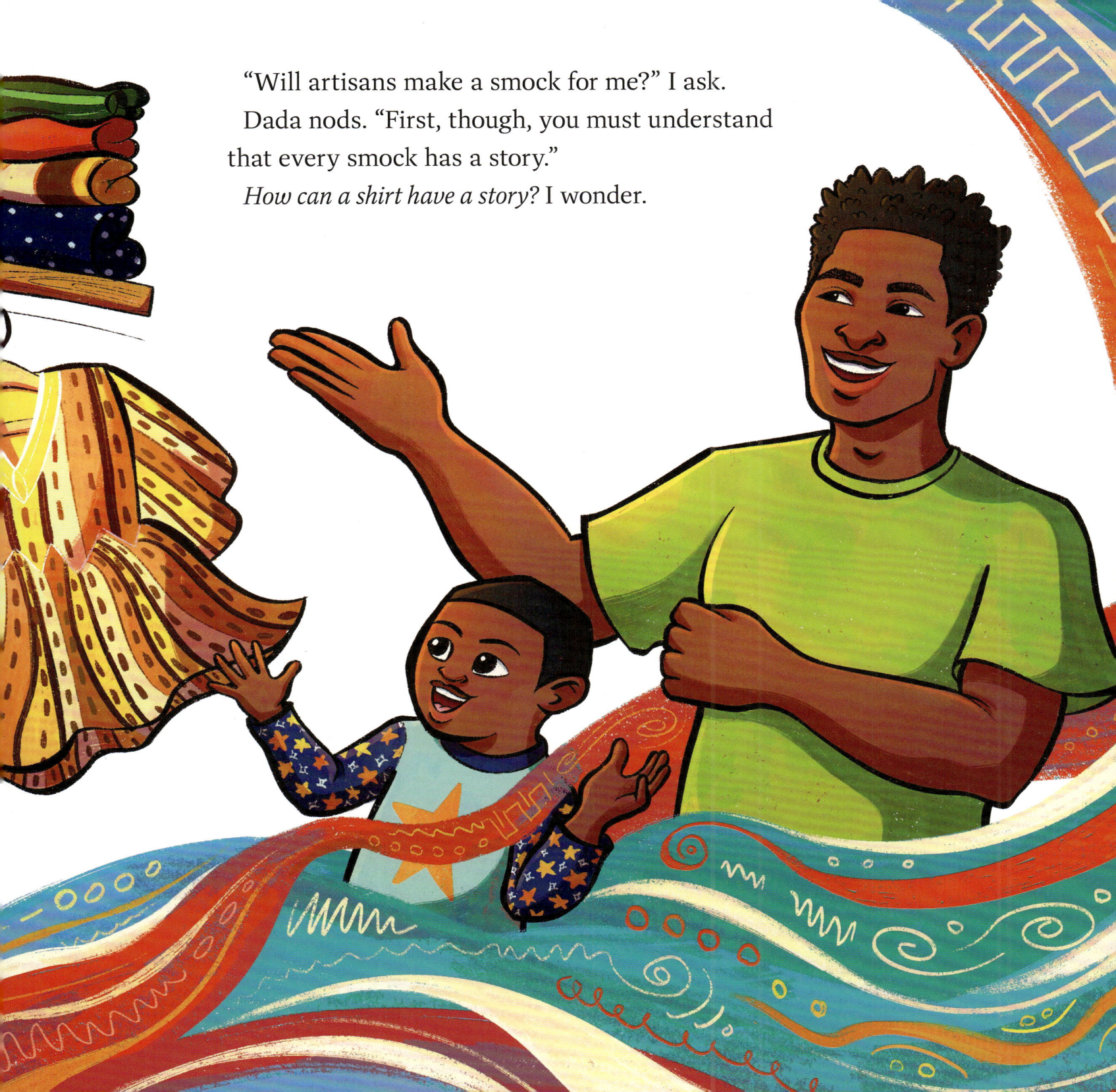

"Will artisans make a smock for me?" I ask.

Dada nods. "First, though, you must understand that every smock has a story."

How can a shirt have a story? I wonder.

"I wore this smock when my uncle became caretaker of the Jena skin," Dada says.
I bow to a line of imaginary elders.

"I played a talking drum in this smock to celebrate a good harvest." I pat the air. *Ga-gong-gong.*

"I wore this smock at my grandmother's funeral to send her off to our ancestors." I imagine standing with Dada to say goodbye. "What about me?" I ask. "Will my smock have a story like yours?"

"In time," Dada says, and squeezes my shoulders.

"Nabila," he continues, "my little chief. You have a very important job today."

"What is it?"

"You will lead the wedding procession."

My eyes grow wide. *Me? In front?*

Dada pats my shoulder. "You are ready," he says.

My stomach flips and flops. "But don't I need my smock?"

"Wait here," he says.

I can't wait! I tug one of Dada's smocks down. *Thump!*
It smells like rain clouds and dusty paths.

Ooof! It weighs me down.

I have to push the fabric forward with my knees. *Shuffle, shuffle, swish.* It drags on the carpet.

I hope my smock smells like rain and dust. When I wear it, everyone will know who I am and that I am Dagomba.

Will my smock make me as proud as Dada felt as the keeper of the Jena skin?

As joyful as a harvest dancer?

As somber as mourners at a funeral?
I hope my smock's story makes Dada proud.

"Here it is!" says Dada. "Your smock. It came all the way from Ghana."

We untie the strings. Unwrap the paper. And unfold . . .

. . . my binŋmaa!

Dada helps me slip the smock over my head.
My smock is not heavy. It sits just right, like two birds on my shoulders.
It is easy to stand proud.

I can jump, jump, spin.
And it smells fresh, like sunshine and dried grass.
I smooth the front of my smock. Dada was right. I am ready to lead the way.

At Auntie's wedding, I watch my family line up. Each smock is different.

"Look at Grandpa's smock," says Dada. "Bright white means power and joy."

I look down. My smock is woven with black, red, and orange.

"Long sleeves mean royalty," Dada continues. "Kings must fold their arms to keep their sleeves off the ground."

My sleeves are short.

"Elder chiefs are proud to wear old smocks," Dada says. "Old means wisdom."

I grin. My smock is brand-new. In it, I will become wise, like Dada.

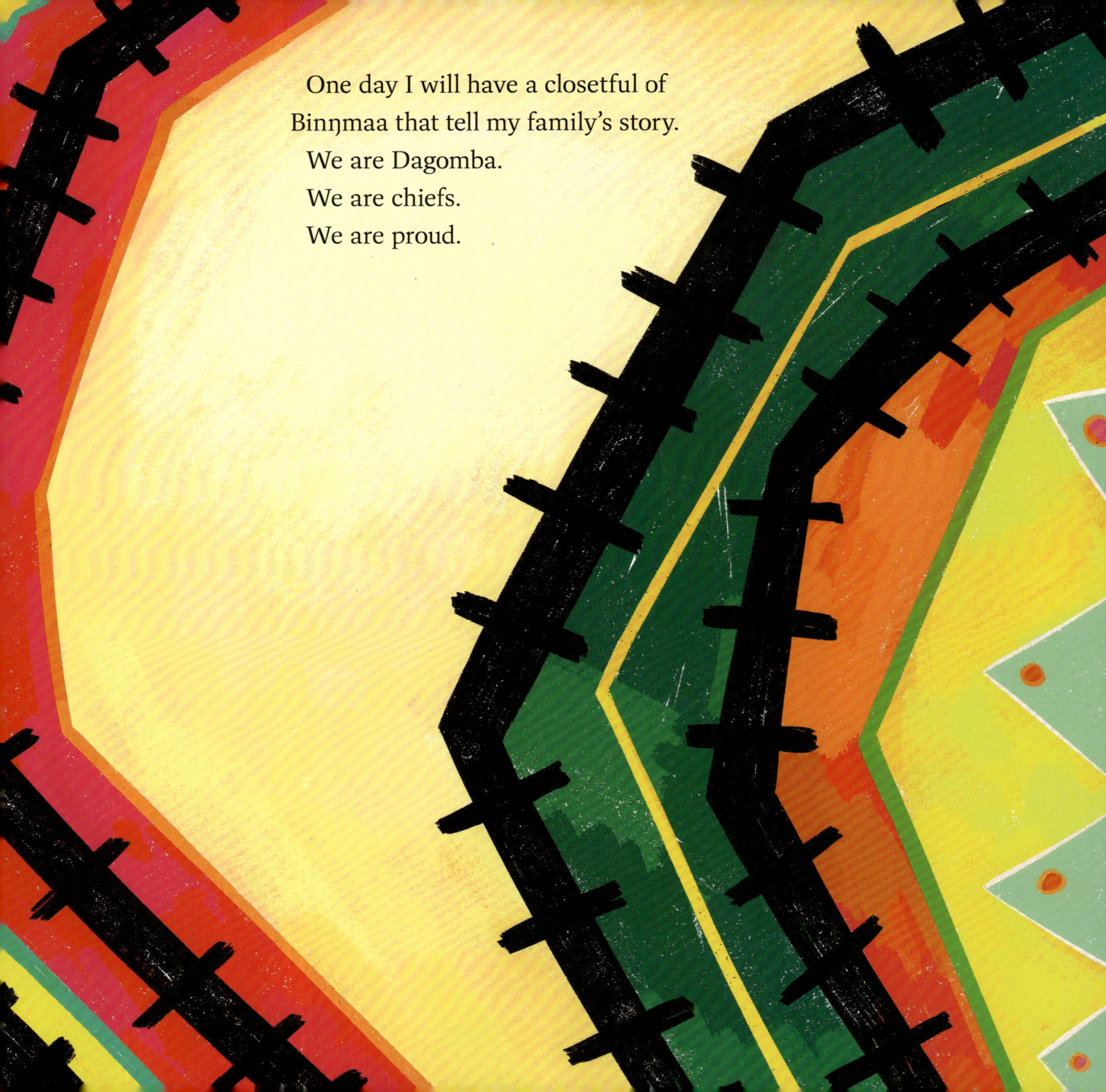

One day I will have a closetful of
Binŋmaa that tell my family's story.
We are Dagomba.
We are chiefs.
We are proud.

Ga-gong-gong. Uncle raps on the talking drum. My stomach feels like it will float away. I hold tight to the hem of my binŋmaa.

Dada hands me a small leather square, an amulet.
"When I was a boy, Grandpa gave me this for protection," he whispers. "Keep it with your smock to give you courage."
I can feel its weight in my pocket, as comforting as Dada's hand on my shoulder.

Ga-gong-gong. I start down the aisle.

Step . . . step . . .

My smock swishes and swings at my hips.

I dance my feet in time with my smock, and I am confident.

Step! Step! Step!

At the front, I turn around. Dada and the rest of the men line up beside me.

When Auntie reaches me, she leans down.

"Nabila," she whispers.

My story starts with a kiss from Auntie.

My story continues surrounded by family.
Stomp-thump-thump.
My smock billows out.
It floats, light as a cloud.

Step-step-bow. Step-step-bow.

Dada tosses me in the air.

My smock is like a parachute, catching me on the way down.

"I'm proud of you, my little chief," Dada whispers.

"In my binŋmaa," I sing.

That night, I fall asleep remembering
cloth perched like a bird on my shoulder—
striding, confident, down the aisle,
standing proud next to Dada,
a kiss from Auntie,
step-step-bow with the uncles.
"Nabila," I whisper, my heart bursting
with pride.

With my smock, my story has begun.

A Ghanaian binŋmaa, or smock, is a striped, tunic-like shirt worn by men in Ghana. Smocks are worn to celebrate rituals, such as weddings, funerals, infant-welcoming ceremonies, and festivals, like the Damba festival, which celebrates the chieftaincy. The smock has been worn by people in the Dagomba tribe for centuries.

The Dagomba tribe lives in northern Ghana. Their smocks are known for being made of coarse, heavy fabrics with front pockets.

In the Dagomba tribe, the ruler over a region is a king. Under the king are chiefs. Princes are the sons of chiefs. Traditionally, smocks have been worn by chiefs and kings. Today, they are worn by people all over Ghana and around the world.

When a Dagomba chief dies, the chief's firstborn son takes over as keeper of that position until a new chief is chosen. During that time, he is a caretaker, not a full chief. The chief position is represented by the skin, so sitting on a sheepskin shows everyone who is the chief. Chiefs preside over a town or area, so the chief of Jena sits on the Jena skin.

Even today, smocks are handmade, typically by women who work together. They sew strips of cotton cloth that are made on a loom into fabric. This gives the smock a plaid appearance. Smocks are often embroidered with white thread.

The leather square that Dada gave his son is an amulet, a small token that is thought to give courage or safety from danger. Dagomba men and women keep them in pockets, tie them to smocks, or hang them on necklaces and wear them as symbols of protection.

A talking drum is a drum from West Africa that has an hourglass shape. When it is played, it has a *gong-gong* sound.

Glossary

This book includes some words that are Dagbani, the language that the Dagomba people speak.

Nabila (nab-i-la) means "little chief."

Binŋmaa (binn-ma) is the Dagbani word for smock.

Authors' Note

In our family, Dada is from the Dagomba tribe in Tamale, Ghana, where smocks are a traditional clothing item. We live in the United States, so we don't get to attend celebrations in Ghana, but we do have some traditional Ghanaian clothing, including smocks, to celebrate in the United States. We wrote this story to share information about this important garment with our kids.

Our son was a toddler when he got his first smock, all the way from Ghana (2019).

Our family wearing traditional Ghanaian attire for a portrait (2021).

Sources

Acquaah, Samuel, Emmanuel R. K. Amissah, and Patrique de Graft Yankson. "Dress Aesthetics of Smock in Northern Ghana: Form, Function, and Context." *Journal of Textile Engineering & Fashion Technology* 1, no. 2 (2017): 68–77. www.medcraveonline.com/JTEFT/dress-aesthetics-of-smock-in-northern-ghana-form-function-and-context.html.

Doortmont, Michel, Hans-Paul Klijnsma, and Marc Prüst, eds. *Northern Ghana Life: If God Breaks Your Leg, He Will Teach You How to Limp*. Netherlands: Groningen, 2018.

Fusheini, Mumuni Zakaria, Joe Adu-Agyem, and Asante Eric Appau. "Indigenous Aesthetic Qualities Inherent in the Dagoma Bim'manli (Smock) in Northern Region of Ghana." *International Journal of Research and Innovation in Social Science* 3, no. 4 (2019): 237–248.